The Tiara Club

at Diamond Turrets

For Princess Mia
and the wonderful Dunblane Library
VF
With very special thanks to JD

ORCHARD BOOKS
338 Euston Road, London NW1 3BH
Orchard Books Australia
Level 17/207 Kent St, Sydney, NSW 2000

A Paperback Original
First published in Great Britain in 2009
Text © Vivian French 2009
Cover illustration © Sarah Gibb 2009
Inside illustrations © Orchard Books 2009

The right of Vivian French to be identified as the author of this
work has been asserted by her in accordance with the Copyright,
Designs and Patents Act 1988.

A CIP catalogue record for this book is available
from the British Library.

ISBN 978 1 84616 875 8

3 5 7 9 10 8 6 4

Printed in Great Britain

Orchard Books is a division of Hachette Children's Books,
an Hachette UK company

www.hachette.co.uk

www.hachettechildrens.co.uk

The Tiara Club
at Diamond Turrets

Princess Mia
and the Magical Koala

By Vivian French

ORCHARD BOOKS

The Royal Palace Academy
for the Preparation of Perfect Princesses

(Known to our students as "The Princess Academy")

OUR SCHOOL MOTTO:
A Perfect Princess always thinks of others
before herself, and is kind, caring and truthful.

Diamond Turrets offers a complete education for
Tiara Club princesses, focusing on caring for animals
and the environment. The curriculum includes:

A visit to the Royal
County Show

Visits to the Country
Park and Bamboo Grove

Work experience on our
very own farm

Elephant rides in our
Safari Park (students will
be closely supervised)

Our headteacher, King Percy, is present at all times, and
students are well looked after by Fairy G, the school
Fairy Godmother.
Our resident staff and visiting experts include:

LADY WHITSTABLE-KENT
(IN CHARGE OF THE FARM,
COUNTRY PARK AND SAFARI PARK)

QUEEN MOTHER MATILDA
(ETIQUETTE, POSTURE AND
APPEARANCE)

FAIRY ANGORA
(ASSISTANT FAIRY GODMOTHER)

FARMER KATE
(DOMESTIC ANIMALS)

LADY MAY (SUPERVISOR OF THE
HOLIDAY HOME FOR PETS)

We award tiara points to encourage our Tiara Club princesses towards the next level. All princesses who win enough points at Diamond Turrets will be presented with their Diamond Sashes and attend a celebration ball.

Diamond Sash Tiara Club princesses are invited to return to Golden Gates, our magnificent mansion residence for Perfect Princesses, where they may continue their education at a higher level.

PLEASE NOTE:
Princesses are expected to arrive at
the Academy with a minimum of:

TWENTY BALLGOWNS
(with all necessary hoops,
petticoats, etc)

TWELVE DAY DRESSES

SEVEN GOWNS
suitable for garden parties
and other special
day occasions

TWELVE TIARAS

DANCING SHOES
five pairs

VELVET SLIPPERS
three pairs

RIDING BOOTS
two pairs

Wellington boots,
waterproof cloaks and other
essential protective clothing
as required

Hi there - and isn't it SO exciting?
We're at Diamond Turrets at
last - and all of us in Tulip Room are
really, REALLY pleased you're here too.
Oh! I'm so silly! I haven't told
you who I am! I'm Princess Mia,
and I share Tulip Room with
Bethany, Caitlin, Lindsey, Abigail and
Rebecca - we've been best friends
for ever. Do you love animals?
I do, and that's why I'm SO
pleased to be here...

Chapter One

I've always loved animals. My mum and dad get SO cross with me, because I'm always smuggling lost kittens or hedgehogs or frogs into my bedroom. Once I rescued a nest of baby mice, and when my mum found them in my wardrobe she screamed so loudly my dad sent six soldiers running to save her!

My auntie, Queen Elisabetta, travels all the time and she adores the animals she meets; it's weird that my mum is always scared. She and Aunt Elisabetta are sisters, after all – I don't know how they could be so different.

So you'll understand why I just couldn't wait to get to Diamond Turrets. My dad told me that the headteacher, King Percy, thinks princesses should know how to look after animals as well as people. "It'll be very good for you, Mia," my dad went on. "You'll learn a lot. There's a wildlife park as well as the home farm – and

I believe there's a place where people can board their pets when they're away on holiday."

"Can I take Whiskers with me?" I asked hopefully, but my dad shook his head.

"There'll be plenty of animals at Diamond Turrets," he said firmly. "And cats don't like travelling if they're not used to it."

I knew that my dad was right, so I didn't try to argue with him. I rushed upstairs to make sure I had everything I needed in my trunk. It all looked fine, and I zoomed back down to the stables. I absolutely had to say goodbye to every single one of the ponies and the horses, and the kitten in the hayloft, and the stable boy's dog...

"Mia!" My dad was sounding cross, so I hurried back again. Our travelling coach was in the courtyard, and my trunks were piled up on the roof. I suddenly realised I must have been much, MUCH longer than I meant to be.

"Ooops," I said. "I'm really sorry!"

My dad sighed heavily. "Maybe you'll learn to behave more like a Perfect Princess this term," he said. "Do try to stop rushing everywhere, Mia!"

I promised, and kissed him goodbye, and then my mum came

sailing out carrying a basket.

"REALLY, Mia!" She frowned at me, which I didn't think was very nice of her. After all, I was just about to go off to school. "You'd forgotten your hair brush, your toothbrush, your pyjamas AND your best tiara! What WERE you thinking of?"

"Animals," my dad said, but there was a twinkle in his eye so I knew he wasn't cross any more. "Let's hope King Percy and Lady Whitstable-Kent can cope with you. I know we can't!"

"Who's Lady...what did you say?" I asked.

"Lady Whitstable-Kent," my dad explained. "She looks after everything. I'm sure you'll like her."

And then my mum put the basket beside me, and gave me a hug...and she and my dad stood waving as the coach trundled out of the courtyard. I was on my way to Diamond Turrets at last!

*

Emerald Castle had been a proper castle on a hill above the sea, and I'd thought Diamond Turrets would be the same – but it wasn't at all. There was a long driveway up through a country park, and I got wildly excited

because I thought I saw a lion,
but Frank, the footman, said
it was only a cow. Then we
passed some farm buildings, and
finally we drove up in front
of a low white building covered
in bright pink roses with little
sparkly turrets at either end.

The front door was wide open, but I could see no sign of any other princesses. In fact, the whole place looked deserted.

Frank opened the coach door and I got out and thanked him. I walked towards the front door wondering if I had arrived on the wrong day. It would be typical of me if I had.

Chapter Two

Frank and the coach driver unloaded my trunks onto the front step, and Frank asked if I was OK.

"Yes, thanks," I said, although I wasn't sure. What if nobody was there? "I'll...I'll go and have a look inside."

"We will be waiting here, Your Highness," Frank said, and I was

SO relieved. I left my basket with my trunks, and ran through the open door – and saw another door in front of me. It had glass panels, and when I peeped through I could see our lovely fairy godmother, Fairy G, and rows and rows of

princesses. They were listening to a tall horsey-looking woman on a stage.

Phew! I thought. *That must be Lady Whitstable-Kent!*

I rushed to tell Frank it was all right before flying back to the hall and pulling at one of the glass doors. At first it wouldn't budge, so I took a deep breath and HEAVED – and it opened with the LOUDEST squeak ever. Lady Whitstable-Kent stopped talking and stared at me, and every single princess turned round to see what was going on.

"Oops," I said, and curtsied. "I'm

so sorry..." And I headed for the nearest empty chair.

It was just my luck that it was next to Diamonde, one of the horrible twins. As I sat down she turned up her nose and hissed, "You're late! Lady Whit started ages ago!"

"I didn't mean to be late," I whispered back. "Is that what

we're meant to call her? Lady Whit?
What's she been saying?"

But Diamonde wouldn't tell me.
She just acted as if I wasn't there.
Lady Whit leant towards Fairy G
and I'm sure she was asking who
I was, because Fairy G looked in
my direction before she answered.
She must have said something nice,

though, because Lady Whit smiled.

"Welcome to our latecomer, Princess Mia!" she said, and she sounded so friendly I heaved a sigh of relief. "Fairy G tells me you are likely to be one of our star pupils. She says you ADORE animals!"

I stood up and curtsied again. "Oh – YES! I really DO!"

"Good!" Lady Whit beamed at me. "Now, one last welcome to everybody on behalf of myself and King Percy – and we do hope you enjoy your time here at Diamond Turrets!" She sat down with a flump as we clapped enthusiastically.

"Ooooh!" Diamonde sneered as we got up to go. "A star pupil, are you, Mia? Huh! I DON'T think so!" And she walked away with the snootiest look on her face.

Of course I absolutely RUSHED to find my friends, and we spent at least ten minutes hugging each other and swapping stories about the holidays. Bethany had been on a royal tour with her parents, and she said she was SO pleased she was back at school and didn't have to get into a horrible rattly coach every day.

"Maybe we should have lessons in 'How to Make a Coach More Comfortable'?" Caitlin suggested.

"Quite right," Rebecca agreed. "'Soft Fluffy Cushions, and How to Create Them!'"

Abigail began to giggle. "Just imagine what Queen Mother Matilda would say! 'A Perfect Princess NEVER complains!'"

"My grandfather once put me

in a coach in my wheelchair," Lindsey said, "and every time we went round a corner I rolled from one side to the other and squashed poor Grandma's toes. She complained like mad!"

Even though we felt sorry for Lindsey's grandmother we couldn't

help laughing as we went off down
the corridor for lunch. We were
hoping we'd be allowed outside
afterwards to have a look round,
and we were thrilled when Fairy G
came stomping in to announce we

had the afternoon free.

"Can we really go anywhere we want?" Rebecca asked.

"More or less," Fairy G told her. "Of course you mustn't go into the Safari Park, but that's a long

way away. And the Enclosure for
Exotic Animals is out of bounds,
but you can explore the farm, and
the country park. Oh – and try
to collect some flowers and leaves
if you can. Tomorrow I'm giving
a lesson on making floral tiaras, and
you'll be expected to wear yours at
the Saturday Party."

We looked at each other in
excitement. A party! And the term
had only just begun!

"Does Lady Whitstable-Kent
let us have a lot of parties?" Lindsey
wanted to know.

Fairy G laughed her huge
booming laugh. "Lady Whit's

not bothered with parties! But King Percy wants you to be Perfect Princesses in every way. You may be working with animals, but you mustn't forget how to behave at a ball. Now, off you go, and make sure you're ready for tea at five o'clock."

Chapter Three

As soon as we'd cleared away our plates we hurried outside. It was a gorgeous sunny day, and first we looked round all the farm buildings. There were lots of flagstone paths, so Lindsey didn't have a problem getting around, and there was something exciting wherever we looked. Chickens were clucking in the yard, and ducks were swimming on the pond behind the stables. There were goats, and pigs, and sheep, and lots of cows – and the sweetest little calf.

We spent so long looking round

the farm we didn't have time to go into the country park, but Caitlin reminded us that there wasn't any hurry. We were going to be there for a whole term, after all!

We made it back to the main

building just in time for tea, and everyone was looking really happy – even the twins. We sat ourselves down, but before we could begin Lady Whit came marching into the dining hall.

"Princesses! DO listen! SUCH a marvellous thing!" She turned to wave at me. "Princess Mia's aunt, who absolutely adores animals, has sent us all a surprise! Not even Mia knows about it. It's a... KOALA! The little thing needs extra special care, and Princess Mia's aunt thought we could look after it until it's strong enough to be returned to the wild. Isn't that wonderful? Let's all give Princess Mia a great big clap!"

Diamonde and Gruella's faces were amazing. Their mouths fell wide open in disbelief.

Apparently the koala had arrived

while we were looking round the farm. I was hoping we could go and see it at once, but Lady Whit said it had to be given a chance to settle quietly into the Reception Clinic. She said we could have a little peek in a day or two if it had started eating and looked happy, but nobody was to go near it until then.

"I suppose you think you're really special because your aunt sends animals here," Diamonde sneered as Lady Whit walked out of the room.

"Actually, no I don't." I helped myself to a large piece of bread and butter. "I think I'm lucky to be here, and I'm pleased Aunt Elisabetta sent the koala so we can all help look after it."

Diamonde looked as if she was

about to say something nasty back, but Rebecca interrupted her.

"Oh NO! I've just thought of something! We completely forgot to pick any flowers!"

"WE remembered," Gruella said smugly. "Didn't we, Diamonde? We've got a HUGE bunch upstairs. We're going to have SUCH pretty tiaras!"

Diamonde smiled her most superior smile. "Oh dear! Are Tulip Room going to be in trouble? WHAT a shame!"

"Maybe we can go out after tea," Lindsey suggested, and we decided that's what we'd do... But after tea

we had to go and unpack. As usual
we chatted so much it took us ages,
and by the time our beautiful new
Tulip Room was tidy it was too late
to go outside.

"We could go early in the
morning," Bethany said as she hung

up her dressing gown.

"Ooof!" Abigail made a face. "Not TOO early, I hope."

Rebecca picked up her alarm clock. "I'll set it for quarter to seven," she said. "Is that OK?"

We all agreed...and Rebecca set her clock.

Chapter Four

When the alarm went off the following morning I almost didn't get up. I was SO comfy and cosy, but Caitlin and Rebecca pulled my covers off, and I staggered out of bed. We got dressed as quickly as we could and tiptoed out of Tulip Room and along the corridor. I thought it felt odd not having any stairs to go down, but Lindsey was grinning as she whizzed along.

The front door was open and we hurried out into the sunshine. There were some very beautiful flowers growing in front of the Reception Clinic, so we headed that

way – and we had just arrived when Abigail grabbed my arm.

"Look!" she said. "The twins!"

She was right. The twins were creeping round the far side of the building, and as we stood and stared we saw them opening a door, and tiptoeing inside.

"Whatever are they doing?" Bethany asked me. "We're not supposed to go near the—"

She never finished her sentence, because there was a loud scream from inside the clinic.

"QUICK!" I said, and we ran. Lindsey got there first, and swung open the door – and there was Diamonde in floods of tears. Behind her was a large airy cage; the koala was crouching down in a corner.

"It scratched me!" Diamonde wailed. "I only wanted to give it a little stroke through the bars!"

I was horrified. How could

she have been so silly? "But it's
a wild animal," I said. "It's not used
to humans!"

Lindsey peered at the scratch on Diamonde's arm, while Gruella stood beside her sister looking worried. "It's only a tiny scratch," Lindsey reported. "It's not even bleeding."

Diamonde went on wailing, and I began to get cross. "Do be quiet!" I snapped. "You'll upset the poor koala. We should go away and leave it alone. It's only tiny, and it probably wants to sleep."

"Oh! Princess-Mia-know-it-all!" Diamonde pulled out her hankie and blew her nose. "Come on, Gruella. We don't want to play with the stupid koala anyway, do we?" And she took her sister's arm and flounced off. Rebecca, Abigail, Caitlin and Lindsey followed them, and Bethany and I were about to go too when I noticed the koala looking at me.

"It's OK, dear little thing," I whispered. "We'll leave you in peace. I'll try to make sure you don't get bothered again."

And then I stopped.

The koala was walking towards me, and as it came it left a trail of pawprints behind it on the sandy floor.

SILVER footprints!

I gasped – but before I had time to show Bethany, a loud voice boomed from outside.

"What EXACTLY do you girls think you're doing here?'

Chapter Five

Bethany scurried out, and I was almost through the door when the koala made the strangest noise. It was like a snore mixed up with a loud hiccup, and I spun round to see the little animal had climbed up the eucalyptus branches in his cage. He was right at the top, holding out a spray of leaves to me...and they were silver, just like his pawprints.

"WOW!" I breathed, and I took the leaves very gently. "Thank you so much."

"Harrunk!" said the koala, and I'm ALMOST certain that he winked at me. Then he settled himself in among the branches, yawned, and shut his eyes. I gave him a tiny wave, and tiptoed away.

Outside the clinic, my friends and the twins were standing in a row in front of King Percy. At least, I guessed that was who it was – he was dressed in dirty old breeches and a muddy velvet jacket, but he wore a crown covered in rubies and diamonds.

"Ha!" he said as I hurried to join them. "Could you please explain what YOU were doing in the Reception Clinic, young lady?"

At once Diamonde stepped

forward. "Princess Mia was trying to stroke the poor little koala, Your Majesty." She shook her head sadly. "Gruella and I did tell her not to, but she wouldn't listen. I'm afraid Mia doesn't always—"

"Silence!" King Percy's eyes flashed. "I don't want to hear such

tales! Princess Mia, please speak for yourself."

"If you please, Your Majesty," I said, "I was about to come out with the others, but then the koala gave me these." And I held out the silver leaves.

King Percy took the leaves and

looked at them. "I see..." he said. "Hmm. It would appear that this koala is no ordinary bear."

Do you ever rush in and say something without thinking? I do – especially when I'm a bit nervous.

"They aren't bears. They're marsupials," I said, and then I blushed bright red and bit my lip. "Oh! I'm SO sorry, Your Majesty! That was VERY rude of me!" I curtsied down to the ground, still blushing, but King Percy burst into peals of laughter.

"You're quite right, of course," he said. "Well done, Princess

Mia!" But then he looked much more serious. "But I still don't understand why you went into the clinic in the first place. Lady Whitstable-Kent definitely informed you all that the koala needed peace and quiet."

"I told you why!" Diamonde

couldn't bear being ignored any longer. "Mia wanted to stroke the koala! And her friends went with her, so Gruella and I went after them to tell them not to. Didn't we, Gruella?"

Gruella hesitated for a moment, and Diamonde elbowed her sharply. "I said, 'Didn't we?'"

Gruella nodded, and King Percy began to frown.

"Is that true?" he asked me.

I didn't know what to say. I couldn't just turn round and accuse Diamonde and Gruella of lying – but then Lindsey pushed her wheelchair forward. Calmly she asked, "Is your arm feeling better now, Diamonde?" She turned to King Percy. "Poor Diamonde. She's got a horrid scratch, but she's being VERY brave."

Diamonde looked SO pleased. "Yes, I am! And it's still sore." She

held up her arm so King Percy could
see.

"Dear me," he said. "And how did
this happen?"

"It was the koala," Gruella

explained. "It didn't like being touched..." And then she squeaked loudly, and covered her mouth with her hand.

*

There was nothing Diamonde could say after that. She had to own up and say she'd been trying to stroke the koala, and King Percy was FURIOUS. He told her she most certainly would NOT be allowed to go to the Saturday Party, and she was given loads of minus tiara points. Gruella didn't get quite so many, but she still looked very fed up.

King Percy gave me back my silver leaves, and we rushed off to pick some flowers for the floral tiara lesson.

We bunched up all our flowers and leaves with the silver leaves, and put them in a jam jar in Tulip Room while we went to have our breakfast. And then the WEIRDEST thing happened!

After breakfast Caitlin and I scurried back to fetch the leaves and flowers... AND THEY'D ALL

TURNED TO SILVER! They looked utterly amazing, and when it was time for our lesson, our tiaras were far and away the prettiest.

Is that boastful? I think it is. I'm very sorry...but Fairy G did agree with me. She said as a reward we could dance the first dance at the Saturday Party all by ourselves, and we were SO thrilled!

Chapter Six

And what happened to the magical koala?

Lady Whitstable-Kent allowed me and my friends to go and see him as soon as he was moved to a bigger enclosure, where there were loads of eucalyptus trees for him to climb and he could feel more as if he was in the wild.

He spent an awful lot of his time asleep, but when he did wake up he'd sometimes come and look at us. Once when we went to see him he'd turned a whole tree silver during the night, but I don't think he meant to. He still looked quite scared and small.

"Will he be all right when he goes back to where he came from?" I asked King Percy, who had come with us.

He nodded. "He'll probably lose his magic powers as he grows older," he said. "But if he doesn't, he'll have learnt how to keep himself safe. That's why your aunt sent him here, of course. Just imagine what greedy people would do if they thought they'd found an animal who could transform ordinary things into silver!"

"OH," I said. "I hadn't thought of that..."

*

And the Saturday Party? It was HUGE fun! The Diamond Turrets ballroom was massive, and Fairy G had decorated it with garlands of leaves and flowers – just like our

floral tiaras! She must have used
magic, as the flowers stayed fresh
and pretty all evening. All of us from
Tulip Room whirled and twirled
round and round until we were
giddy...

And when we went to bed that night I thought I'd never get to sleep.

"Isn't it FUN here?" I whispered after Fairy G had been in to turn our light off. "Don't you think Diamond Turrets is the best place ever?"

But do you know what?

All my friends were fast asleep already, so I thought I'd say goodnight to you instead.

Goodnight, special friend. See you soon!

Don't miss  website at:

www.tiaraclub.co.uk

Keep up to date with the latest
Tiara Club books and meet all
your favourite princesses!

There is SO much to see and do,
including games and activities. You can
even become an exclusive member of the
Tiara Club Princess Academy.

PLUS, there are exciting
competitions with truly
FABULOUS prizes!

Be a Perfect Princess – check it out today!

What happens next?
Find out in

Princess Bethany
and the Lost Piglet

A farming we will go...and
I do SO hope you're going to come
with us! I'm Princess Bethany from
Tulip Room, and all my friends - that's
Caitlin, Lindsey, Abigail, Rebecca and
Mia - want me to say that they hope
you come with us, too! It's fun being
here at Diamond Turrets, but do you
know what? Sometimes I get a bit
anxious about all the animals here.
PLEASE don't tell anyone, but I secretly
think cows
are a little bit scary...

I don't think any of us had ever seen our school fairy godmother, Fairy G, wearing rubber boots before – she looked so funny when she came stomping up the path to meet us for our very first farming lesson.

"Do you think she can fly in them?" Caitlin whispered in my ear.

I tried not to giggle. It's a little bit difficult to think of Fairy G flying, actually. She isn't exactly fairy shaped – not like her assistant, Fairy Angora. Fairy Angora is very slim and pretty, but Fairy G is…I can't think of the right word without sounding rude. Comfortable, perhaps. But she's SO lovely, and she looks after us brilliantly.

"Now, princesses," she boomed. "You've got a wonderful morning ahead of you! Farmer Kate is going to take us to see the piglets, and after that she'll show you how to feed the adult pigs."

The twins were standing near us, and I saw them look at each other and roll their eyes. "Yuck! Mummy would NEVER let us go near any horrible smelly pigs," Diamonde said loudly.

Fairy G frowned, and folded her arms. "You should know, Diamonde," she said crossly, "that pigs are extremely clean by nature. Farmer Kate's pigs live out in the orchards most of the time, and they most certainly do NOT smell! Now, please put your boots on, and we'll be off. Follow me, everyone!" And she set off towards the farm.

Diamonde made a face as she looked at the row of rubber boots lined up outside the back door. "If anyone thinks I'm going to wear such nasty clumpy things, they're wrong. 'A Perfect Princess should always look her very best', and I'M a Perfect Princess!" She stuck her nose in the air and walked on down the path, ignoring the boots completely.

"And I'm a Perfect Princess too!" Gruella echoed, as she followed Diamonde.

The Tiara Club books are priced at £3.99. Butterfly Ball, Christmas Wonderland, Princess Parade, Emerald Ball and Midnight Masquerade are priced at £5.99. The Tiara Club books are available from all good bookshops, or can be ordered direct from the publisher: Orchard Books, PO BOX 29, Douglas IM99 IBQ.
Credit card orders please telephone 01624 836000 or fax 01624 837033 or visit our website: www.orchardbooks.co.uk or e-mail: bookshop@enterprise.net for details.

To order please quote title, author and ISBN and your full name and address.
Cheques and postal orders should be made payable to 'Bookpost plc.'
Postage and packing is FREE within the UK
(overseas customers should add £2.00 per book).
Prices and availability are subject to change.